To Keith Harrison, who published these poems first,
and to the memory of Halfdan Rasmussen, who wrote them
M. N. and P. E.

To Jack and Keegan
K. H.

To the memory of Karla Harry,
late school librarian of the Gordon School

Text copyright © 2011 by Halfdan Rasmussen
Translations copyright © 2011 by Marilyn Nelson and Pamela Espeland
Illustrations copyright © 2011 by Kevin Hawkes

First edition 2011

Library of Congress Cataloging-in-Publication Data

Rasmussen, Halfdan Wedel, 1915–2002.
[Poems. English. Selections]
A little bitty man and other poems for the very young / Halfdan Rasmussen ; translated by
Marilyn Nelson and Pamela Espeland ; illustrated by Kevin Hawkes. — 1st ed.
p. cm.
ISBN 978-0-7636-2379-1
1. Children's poetry, Danish—Translations into English. 2. Rasmussen, Halfdan Wedel, 1915–2002.
Translations into English. I. Nelson, Marilyn, date. II. Espeland, Pamela, date.
III. Hawkes, Kevin. IV. Title.

PT8175.R33A6 2010
831'.914—dc22

2009007515

11 12 13 14 15 16 CCP 10 9 8 7 6 5 4 3 2 1
Printed in Shenzhen, Guangdong, China

This book was typeset in Bembo Educational.
The illustrations were done in acrylic and charcoal pencil.

Candlewick Press
99 Dover Street
Somerville, Massachusetts 02144

visit us at www.candlewick.com

A Little Bitty Man

and Other Poems for the Very Young

HALFDAN RASMUSSEN

translated by
MARILYN NELSON & PAMELA ESPELAND

illustrated by
KEVIN HAWKES

Candlewick Press

Contents

A Little Bitty Man

A little bitty man

took a ride on a snail

down a little bitty road that was shady.

The little bitty man

came to Littlebittyland,

where he married a little bitty lady.

The little bitty man

bought a little bitty house

for a little bit of little bitty money.

The little bitty lady

grew very, very big

with a little bitty baby in her tummy.

What Things Are For

Nails are to pound on

and hammers to pound with.

Paths are to walk on

and friends are to walk with.

Knees are to crawl on,

bottoms to fall on.

Sleds are to slide on,

    ponies to ride on.

Feet are to jump on,

    drums are to thump on.

Tiptoes to snoop on,

    and potties to poop on!

A Miracle

A ball bounced high into the air.

A curious frog sat up to stare.

He thought, "A miracle! How neat!

It hops, but it ain't got feet!"

The Elf

The elf puts on his winter coat

and puts his winter hat on,

finds a muffler for his throat

in his drawer—puts that on,

packs his pockets full of mice

and then, before he goes,

puts on an empty ice-cream cone

to insulate his nose.

What Comes Next

First come the schoolboys with bare knees and feet,

and then come young girls with spring flowers.

Then come the plows and the planters of wheat,

and then come the clouds and the showers.

Then come the pastures with slow, placid cows,

and then comes the meadowlark's trill.

Then come the harvesters wiping their brows,
and then comes the grain to the mill.

Then comes the wind so the windmill can go,
and then come the mice to partake.

Then come the children to play in the snow,
and then come the bakers with cake.

You Can Pat My Pet

You can pat

my dog for a dime

and my horse

for an egg and a half.

You can pat

my favorite aunt

if you give me

your granddad's moustache.

You can pat my goldfish's hair

for an apple

that's polished just right.

But if you want

to pat my lion,

just promise

you'll pat it *real light*!

Emergency

Ben's britches are burning!
"Water, quick!" cries Don—
because first thing this morning
Don put Ben's britches on!

Dr. Dorothy

When Dorothy told her dolly,

"You look so pale today

I'll have to give you medicine!"

—her dolly ran away!

Those Fierce Grown-up Soldiers

Those fierce grown-up soldiers

who shoot guns and fight

should learn from us children

to fight a war right.

First, fight with toy guns.

Then, if your war won't end,

you tickle your enemy

into a friend!

Little Cloud

Little Cloud went for a walk
above the highest steeple,
cast a shadow on a wall,
looked down at the people.

Looked into a little lake,

saw its own reflection,

saw a duck that swam around

in every which direction.

Couldn't hold it anymore,

didn't have a potty.

Let it drip down on the road,

knew that it was naughty.

Ran home with the wind again,

past mountaintops with snow on,

Got a scolding from its mom

and put some drier clothes on.

Days

Poor old blue Monday
with plumes in his cap
met up with Tuesday,
a likable chap.

Wednesday came whimpering
after this pair,
and lonesome gray Thursday
with snarls in her hair.

Friday and Saturday
drove laughing past
with a basket of goodies
to eat on the grass.

Then Sunday went out

and took off his shoes

and forgot about

Monday

and Tuesday

and Wednesday

and Thursday

and Friday

and Saturday

and snoozed!

The Strange Old Owl

The strange old owl awakens

in the middle of the night,

looks up at the moon

that's already out of sight,

polishes his glasses,

gives the cat a wink,

and writes these silly poems

with invisible ink.

Peter & Patrick & Powell

Peter and Patrick and Powell
dug a deep hole with a trowel.

It was deeper, that hole, by a meter
than Patrick and Powell and Peter.

A goat came, before these three knew it,

and butted them all right into it.

And that, I'm afraid, was the last trick

of Powell and Peter and Patrick.